D0276111

Class No. ___J___   Acc No. _C/68910._

Author: _CUNLIFFE, J._   Loc: _/ / JUN 1997_

LEABHARLANN
CHONDAE AN CHABHAIN

1. This book may be kept three weeks.
    It is to be returned on / before the last date
    stamped below.
2. A fine of 20p will be charged for every week
    or part of week a book is overdue.

The New Adventures of Postman Pat

Postman Pat™

paints the ceiling

Cavan County Library

Withdrawn Stock

John Cunliffe
Illustrated by Stuart Trotter

from the original television designs by **Ivor Wood**

*Hodder
Children's
Books*

a division of Hodder Headline plc

More Postman Pat adventures:

Postman Pat and the hole in the road
Postman Pat and the suit of armour
Postman Pat in a muddle
Postman Pat misses the show
Postman Pat follows a trail
Postman Pat has the best village
Postman Pat has too many parcels

First published 1997
by Hodder Children's Books,
a division of Hodder Headline plc,
338 Euston Road, London NW1 3BH

Story copyright © 1997 Ivor Wood and John Cunliffe
Text copyright © 1997 John Cunliffe
Illustrations copyright © 1997 Hodder Children's Books
and Woodland Animations Ltd.

ISBN 0 340 678119
10 9 8 7 6 5 4 3 2 1

A catalogue record for this book is available
from the British Library.
The right of John Cunliffe to be identified as the
Author of this Work has been asserted by him.

All rights reserved.

Printed in Italy.

CAVAN COUNTY LIBRARY
ACC. No. ..C16891.0......
CLASS No. ......J......
INVOICE NO. 3668........
PRICE....£7.99.

Here he comes! It's Pat, on his way with the letters, buzzing about
Greendale, as busy as ever. There are some letters for Granny Dryden
today. As Pat comes up the garden path, he can see some pots of paint
on her windowsill.

"Looks as though someone's busy doing a spot of painting," says Pat. "Morning, Granny Dryden!"

There was Granny Dryden, standing on a box, sploshing at the wall with the paint.

"You're making a grand job of that!" said Pat. "It's going to look lovely when you've finished."

"Nay, Pat," said Granny Dryden. "I'll not be able to make a right job of it. That ceiling wants doing, and I'll never reach that in all my days!"

CAVAN COUNTY LIBRARY

"Would you like a hand with it?" said Pat. "I could borrow some ladders and planks from Ted. I'll pop round after work, and do that ceiling for you in two ticks. You might need a drop more paint. Let's have a look - how much is there in this one? I think it's empty!"

Pat tipped one of the paint-pots upside down and gave it a shake.

"Do be careful," said Granny Dryden, "it's messy stuff . . ."
"Oooooh!" said Pat.

A slop of paint came glooping out, and went all down Pat's trousers.

"Now you've gone and done it!" said Granny Dryden. "All down your nice clean trousers! See if you can wipe it off before it soaks in."

She gave him a piece of rag to wipe it with.

"I think it's just making it worse - it's only spreading it out!" said Pat.

"Ooh, I am sorry about your trousers!" said Granny Dryden. "What *is* Sara going to say?"

"Never you worry about that - it was my own fault," said Pat. "I should take more care. I expect *that's* what Sara will say! I'll nip home and change. These are not my best pair, luckily. And I'll put an old pair of jeans on to paint that ceiling."

"Oh, you are kind, Pat," said Granny Dryden. "Now, mind how you go."

Pat was on his way.
It didn't take long to get home.
Sara did get a surprise when she saw him.

"What are you doing back, at this time of day?" she said.
"And what on earth have you done to your trousers?"

"It's only a drop of paint. You see . . ."

He told her all about Granny Dryden's ceiling.

"Well, you can't put your best pair of trousers on for work," said
Sara. "I took them to the cleaners in Pencaster, yesterday, and they
won't be ready till Thursday."

"What am I going to do?" said Pat.

"You could look in the airing-cupboard," said Sara. "I think there's that old pair that you do the gardening in."

"They'll be better than nothing," said Pat. "I'll have a look."

When Sara saw Pat coming downstairs in his old trousers, she couldn't help laughing. He had found a pair of trousers he once wore on holiday, long ago. They didn't fit very well.

"Are they long shorts, or short longs?" she said.

"Nay they'll do, won't they?" said Pat. "I can't hang about any longer, with all these letters to deliver."

He was soon on his way again, with rather chilly knees.
Jess didn't know what to make of Pat's bare knees.
He thought summer must have arrived early.

They called on Miss Hubbard next. She was gathering some flowers for the church. She nearly dropped all her flowers when she saw Pat!

"Oh, goodness me, Pat," she said, "what are you doing in shorts? It's not summer yet. Cast not a clout till May be out!"

"They're not shorts, Miss Hubbard, they're an old pair of trousers. It's Granny Dryden, you see. She's painting her room, and she can't reach the ceiling, and –"

"I don't believe a word of it!" laughed Miss Hubbard. "It's that post-office - they're going all continental - something to do with this Common Market - the 'swinging postman' image - I know all about that! Did you say Granny Dryden was painting? Do you mean a picture?"

"No - she's painting her sitting room," said Pat,
"and I'm going to give a hand with the ceiling."

"Well, I don't know what that's got to do with wearing Bermuda
shorts!" said Miss Hubbard. "It's a funny old world. But, what she will
need is plenty of sheets to cover the furniture."

"Oooh, I don't think she's got many. I didn't see any," said Pat.

"She'll certainly need some sheets if you're going to help her!"
said Miss Hubbard. "I've seen what a man can do with a pot of paint.
I have plenty of old sheets - I'll just get some out of the cupboard
for you."

When Miss Hubbard
came out with the sheets,
the wind took hold of them,
and whirled them about, wrapping them round her.
She whooshed and billowed into the garden.

"Help! A ghost!" shouted Pat. "Is it you, Miss Hubbard?"
A muffled voice came out of the bundle of sheets.
"Don't just stand there! Get me out of this!
Catch hold of that corner, and pull!
Oh, Pat, be careful,
there goes my hat!"

What a struggle
Pat had to disentangle her!
The wind had wrapped her up
like a mummy. When Pat set her free
at last, Miss Hubbard gasped,
"There you are, Pat. Pop these sheets
in your van, and let's have
no more ghosts."

Pat was on his way again.

There was a cold breeze blowing, so he wrapped a sheet round his legs to keep his knees warm.

He called at Ted Glen's workshop. There was no sign of Ted.

"Hello, Ted," shouted Pat, "where are you? Post!"

Pat peered through the window. The workshop was empty.

"Where has he got to?"

Ted was in the garden getting his spring carrots in. When he heard somebody bumping about in his workshop, he thought he'd better go and have a look - you never know - it might be a burglar!

Ted crept very quietly round to the door - and bumped into Pat coming out. "STOP!" shouted Ted, grabbing Pat.

"Oh, help! Ted!" said Pat. "It's me!"

"Sorry, Pat, I thought you were a burglar!" said Ted.

"A house-painter, more like!" said Pat. "I've promised to give Granny Dryden a hand with painting her ceiling. Do you think I could borrow some ladders?"

"I'll do better than that," said Ted. "I'll give you a hand. Are you doing it before you go on holiday?"

"I'm not going on holiday, Ted!"

"I just thought you were wearing the gear!" Ted laughed. "These snazzy shorts! Very smart! I'll meet you tonight, at Granny Dryden's, with the ladders - seven o'clock!"

"Right-o! Thanks a lot, Ted. Cheerio!"

Pat was off again - to Thompson Ground.

Dorothy was tidying up in the yard. When she saw Pat she said, "Oh, it's Pat. I wonder what he's brought today?"

"Lots of letters, today, Dorothy," said Pat. "And it's a right busy day - a touch of Spring in the air, what with you getting all tidied up, and Granny Dryden painting her room."

"I hope she has plenty of paint?"
said Dorothy. "It always takes twice as much
as you think it's going to need."

"Well, she might be a bit short," said Pat.

"Like your trousers?"

"Well, now, that's another story . . ."

"We have plenty of pots in the barn," Dorothy said.
"We always keep a good store - always painting something,
we are - I'm sure we can spare a drop for Granny Dryden.
Just keep a look out for our silly hens - they get everywhere!"

Pat went into the barn to look for the pots of paint. It was very gloomy, and he kept bumping into things.

"Hey up! Ouch! It's a bit dark in here!"

"Try that shelf over there!" said Dorothy.

Pat got hold of a sleepy hen by mistake. It clucked loudly, and flapped its wings.

"Oh, help, a flying paint-pot!"

"It's a new kind. Egg-shell finish!" laughed Dorothy. "I'll wait outside till you've done! I can do without an egg-shell finish on me!"

When Pat came out of the barn he looked really funny. He had feathers all over him, and bits of straw in his hair. Dorothy couldn't help laughing.

It was a busy scene at Granny Dryden's cottage that evening. Ted and Pat rigged up the ladders, and soon got to work, painting the ceiling.

"We'll soon be done! It'll be just like new!" said Ted.

"I think I've about done my bit!" said Pat.

"It looks really lovely," said Ted.

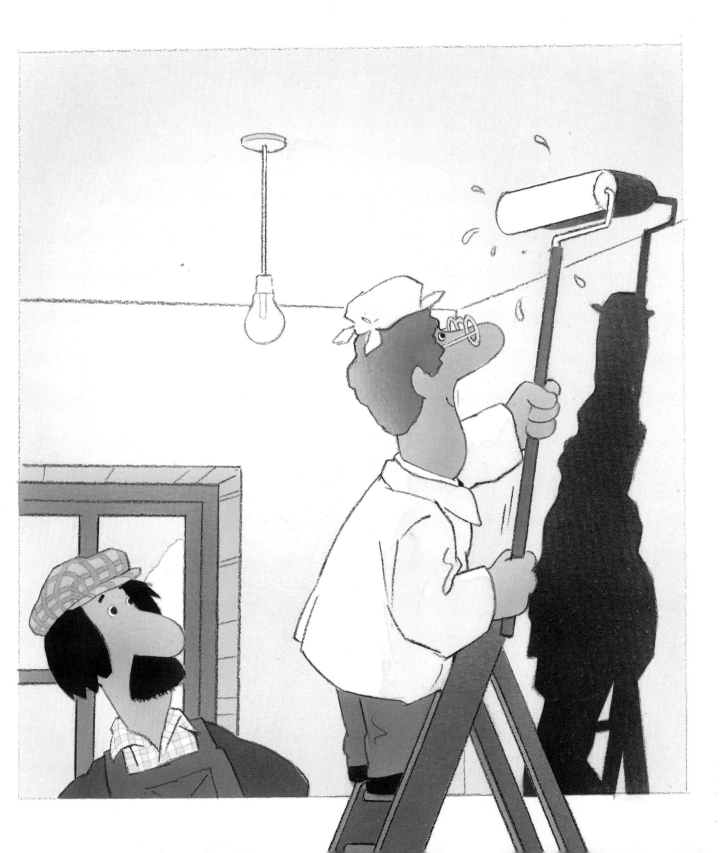

"And I have a surprise for you!" said Granny Dryden, as she came in with a tray of tea. She gazed at her new ceiling. "Oh, it's lovely, it really is, I could never have done it on my own; you are kind."

In the middle of the tea-things, Ted found something odd.

"Here, look at this," said Ted. "I've found another pot of paint!"

"Give it a good stir, before it sets hard!" said Pat.

What a surprise Ted had, when he tried to take the lid off!

"Nay, it isn't a pot of paint at all, it's a cake!"

"A surprise," smiled Granny Dryden. "Just to say 'Thank-you' to you both."

"Now that's the best pot of paint I ever saw," said Pat.
"And it's one you can't spill down your trousers!" said Granny Dryden.

Then they all had a large slice of cake, and a good drink of tea.
When they had packed up the ladders, and folded up the sheets,
and cleaned up the paint-drips, Ted and Pat went home.

Granny Dryden had another cup of tea, and smiled as she looked at her nice new ceiling. It had never looked so good, in all her days!

CAVAN COUNTY LIBRARY